Ethan Long

PRESENTS

FANGSGIVING

WITHDRAWN

BLOOMSBURY
CHILDREN'S BOOKS
NEW YORK LONDON OXFORD NEW DELHI SYDNEY

BLOOMSBURY CHILDREN'S BOOKS
Bloomsbury Publishing Inc., part of Bloomsbury Publishing Plc
1385 Broadway, New York, NY 10018

BLOOMSBURY, BLOOMSBURY CHILDREN'S BOOKS, and the Diana logo are trademarks of Bloomsbury Publishing Plc

First published in the United States of America in September 2018
by Bloomsbury Children's Books

Bloomsbury books may be purchased for business or promotional use. For information on bulk
purchases please contact Macmillan Corporate and Premium Sales Department at
specialmarkets@macmillan.com

Library of Congress Cataloging-in-Publication Data available upon request
LCCN 2017052507 (hardcover) | LCCN 2017060461 (e-book)
ISBN 978-1-68119-825-5 (hardcover) • ISBN 978-1-68119-826-2 (e-book) • 978-1-68119-827-9 (e-PDF)

Art created with graphite pencil on Strathmore drawing paper, then scanned and colorized digitally
Typeset in Sprocket BT
Book design by Ethan Long and Yelena Safronova • Handlettering by Ethan Long
Printed in China by Leo Paper Products, Heshan, Guangdong
2 4 6 8 10 9 7 5 3 1

All papers used by Bloomsbury Publishing Plc are natural, recyclable products
made from wood grown in well-managed forests. The manufacturing processes
conform to the environmental regulations of the country of origin.

To find out more about our authors and books visit www.bloomsbury.com and sign up for our newsletters.

For the witnesses of the pizza incident

It was the fourth Thursday in November and the monsters gathered for their annual Thanksgiving feast.

Everyone chipped in.

Virginia whipped up the sweet-potato casserole.

Sandy mixed the stuffing.

Mumford made the cranberry sauce.

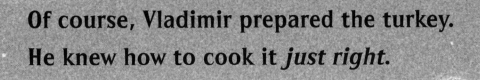

Of course, Vladimir prepared the turkey.
He knew how to cook it *just right*.

Then, out of nowhere,
he heard a

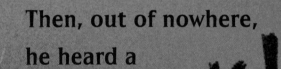

HONK!
HONK!
HONK!

It was a happy reunion.

Vladimir invited them inside.

Uncle Gus inspected the turkey.

Of course, he had his own method.

Now *that's* how you cook a *turkey*!

Joey and Shmoey helped Fran make the pumpkin pie.

But it turned into a *lump*-kin pie.

They just *love* maggot meatballs.

And then there was Spike, who never met *anything* he didn't want to swallow.

Anything.

Vladimir loved his family but they were quickly making a monstrosity of the Thanksgiving feast.

And they didn't stop there. The bean casserole had ten sticks of boogey butter in it, the mashed potatoes had a strange "look" to them, and the biscuits were as hard as headstones.

And the turkey? Let's just say that Uncle Gus cooked it to death.

The room went black.

And when the light went on . . .

Thanksgiving was *gone*!

Dog gone!

Spike had devoured everything!

For Vladimir, this *was* the last straw.

Aunt Bessy was right. They *were* family.

And if Vladimir remembered correctly,
family worked *together*.
So he demanded a do-over.

They cooked all day. They used whatever they could find.
They made potato-peel pudding. They cooked a bread-crust
casserole. They baked turkey-bone biscuits.

WHIRRRRRRR

They even made a batch of flea-bean dip,
with just a touch of garlic.

So on the fourth Friday in November, everyone gave thanks.
Even Spike was grateful, in his own way.

And, of course, the food was to *die* for!